Note to parents, carers and teachers

Read it yourself is a series of modern stories, favourite characters and traditional tales written in a simple way for children who are learning to read. The books can be read independently or as part of a guided reading session.

Each book is carefully structured to include many high-frequency words vital for first reading. The sentences on each page are supported closely by pictures to help with understanding, and to offer lively details to talk about.

The books are graded into four levels that progressively introduce wider vocabulary and longer stories as a reader's ability and confidence grows.

Ideas for use

- Ask how your child would like to approach reading at this stage. Would he prefer to hear you read the story first, or would he like to read the story to you and see how he gets on?

- Help him to sound out any words he does not know.

- Developing readers can be concentrating so hard on the words that they sometimes don't fully grasp the meaning of what they're reading. Answering the puzzle questions on pages 46 and 47 will help with understanding.

For more information and advice on Read it yourself and book banding, visit www.ladybird.com/readityourself

Book
Band
8

Level 3 is ideal for children who are developing reading confidence and stamina, and who are eager to read longer stories with a wider vocabulary.

Special features:

Detailed pictures for added interest and discussion

Wider vocabulary, reinforced through repetition

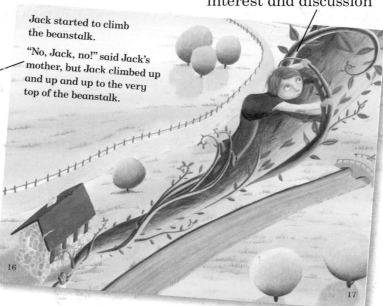

Jack started to climb the beanstalk.

"No, Jack, no!" said Jack's mother, but Jack climbed up and up and up to the very top of the beanstalk.

16

17

Longer sentences

Simple story structure

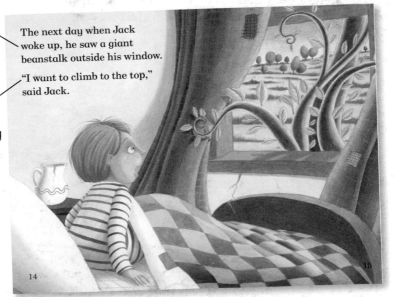

The next day when Jack woke up, he saw a giant beanstalk outside his window.

"I want to climb to the top," said Jack.

14

15

Educational Consultant: Geraldine Taylor
Book Banding Consultant: Kate Ruttle

A catalogue record for this book is available from the British Library

Published by Ladybird Books Ltd
80 Strand, London, WC2R 0RL
A Penguin Company

001

ISBN: 978-0-72327-300-4

Printed in China

Jack and the Beanstalk

Illustrated by Laura Barella

Jack and his mother were very poor. All they had was one cow.

One day, Jack's mother said, "Go and sell our cow and bring the money back to me."

Jack took the cow away to sell.
On the way he met a man who
wanted to buy the cow.

9

"I have no money," said the man.
"But I will give you five magic
beans for your cow."

"All right," said Jack,
and he gave the man his cow.

Jack took the beans back to his mother. She was very angry.

"These beans are no good to us," she said.
And she threw the beans out of the window.

The next day when Jack woke up, he saw a giant beanstalk outside his window.

"I want to climb to the top," said Jack.

Jack started to climb
the beanstalk.

"No, Jack, no!" said Jack's
mother, but Jack climbed up
and up and up to the very
top of the beanstalk.

Jack saw a giant castle with a giant door. When he opened the door he saw a giant woman.

"Look out!" said the woman. "My husband is coming. He will eat you up!"

"Fee-fi-fo-fum, watch out everyone, HERE I COME," roared the giant.

"You must hide," said the woman. And she hid Jack in a cupboard.

The giant came in and sat down at the table with some giant bags of money. He started to count his money. Jack watched him from inside the cupboard.

Soon, the giant
fell asleep. Jack came out
of the cupboard and took all
the money. Then he climbed
down the beanstalk, and gave
the money to his mother.

25

Not long after, Jack wanted to climb the beanstalk again.

"No, Jack, no!" said his mother. But Jack said, "I must."

Jack saw the giant
woman again.

"Look out!" she said.
"My husband is angry because
his money has been stolen."

"Fee-fi-fo-fum, watch out
everyone, HERE I COME!"
roared the giant.

"You must hide in the cupboard," said the woman.

The giant came in and sat down at the table. He had with him a magic hen. The magic hen laid golden eggs.

Very soon, the giant fell
asleep. Jack came out of
the cupboard and took the
hen. Then he climbed down
the beanstalk.

33

The next day, Jack climbed
the beanstalk again.
At the top of the beanstalk,
Jack saw the giant woman.

"Look out!" said the woman. "My husband is angry because his hen and his money have been stolen."

"Fee-fi-fo-fum, watch out everyone, HERE I COME!" roared the giant.

"You must hide in the cupboard again," said the woman.

The giant came in with a magic harp. He sat down at the table and the harp started to play.

Soon, the giant fell asleep. Jack came out of the cupboard and took the harp. Then he started to climb down the beanstalk.

"Run away!" said the woman. "The giant is behind you!"

41

Jack climbed down the beanstalk with the angry giant behind him. When Jack was at the bottom, his mother cut down the beanstalk.

CRASH! And that was the end of the giant.

Now Jack and his mother
were not poor, and they lived
happily ever after.

How much do you remember about the story of Jack and the Beanstalk? Answer these questions and find out!

- How many magic beans are there?

- What does Jack's mother do with the magic beans?

- What is at the top of the beanstalk?

- Where does Jack hide in the castle?

- Can you remember two of the things Jack takes from the giant?

Look at the different story sentences and match them to the people who said them.

"Fee-fi-fo-fum."

"Run away! The giant is behind you!"

"I will give you five magic beans for your cow."

"These beans are no good to us!"

"I want to climb to the top."

Read it yourself with Ladybird

Tick the books you've read!

For more confident readers who can read simple stories with help.

Level 3

☐ ☐

☐ ☐ ☐ ☐ ☐ ☐ ☐

Longer stories for more independent, fluent readers.

Level 4

☐ ☐

☐ ☐ ☐ ☐ ☐ ☐ ☐ ☐

The Read it yourself with Ladybird app is now available for iPad, iPhone and iPod touch

App also available on Android devices